I0830764

Down in the deep, where the bubbles go 'plop,'
Swam fish big and small, they'd flip and they'd flop.
Some danced like stars in a fin-flashing show,
While others told jokes that made sea cucumbers glow!

Some fish did yoga, some lifted weights,
Some fish took selfies on undersea dates!
One fish was vlogging, one fish was mad,
Another just stared at his screen looking sad.

Some fish took naps, some went for a jog,
One fish just argued with an emotional frog.
Some fish had podcasts, some fish sold merch,
One fish just sat there and screamed, 'DO YOUR RESEARCH!'

The ocean was big, the ocean was wide,
And all of the fish swam side by side.
No fish cared about color or name,
No fish needed a 'group' to proclaim!

They played and they partied, they ate, and they laughed,
They never once argued, they never kept track!
No fish was judged for the way that they swam,
No fish got canceled, no fish got banned.

But then came a fish with a wide, thoughtful stare...
And suddenly said, 'Wait... this shit isn't fair!
Why are we mixing?! Why is this so?!
We should be sorted! This ocean must flow!'

The fish all looked up and tilted their heads...
'Um... dude, what? We were just going to bed.
We don't have a problem, we're happy and free!'
'But go off and fuck things up, I guess,' said a fish sipping tea.

One fish looked close at the fish swimming past,
Then gasped and then shouted, 'We've been mixed up too fast!
Why should we swim with fish not like we?!
Shouldn't fish swim in groups that match perfectly?!'

'White fish, come here! Black fish, stand tall!
It's better for us if we don't mix at all!
We need our own schools, our own special way—
Let's split the ocean, starting today!'

The fish were confused. 'Wait—why should we split?'
'Because...' said the fish, 'Uh... it just makes sense, that's it!
We've been too mixed! We've been too free!
We NEED some more rules to fix the deep sea!'

'From now on, fish must stay in their place!
We'll set up new boundaries! We'll measure with SPACE!
No more just swimming all loose and untamed...
From now on, the ocean is SYSTEM-ARRANGED!'

Now two different schools, one dark and one light,
Each swam in their group, believing it right.
'No more mixed waters! No more strange friends!
We stick to OUR kind, and THAT'S where it ends!'

'Wait... I kinda LIKED swimming with Ted...'
Said a fish looking sad, scratching his head.
'TOO BAD BITCH!' said a fish with a megaphone loud,
'We SWIM WITH OUR OWN! It's the rules of the crowd!'

'You there! Stop swimming outside of your lane!
You're breaking the system! You're causing us pain!'
'You're making things worse! You're a terrible trout!'
'APOLOGIZE NOW! Or we're kicking you out!'

Some fish got nervous. Some fish felt small.
Some fish just shrugged and said, 'Fine, whatever, y'all.'
But deep in their gills, a feeling was there...
Like maybe, just maybe, this wasn't so fair...

But THEN came a fish, a fish that was woke,
Who flailed and who ranted, 'You fish are a joke!
You don't see the SYSTEM, the harm and the pain!
You must change your ways, or you'll be to blame!'

'You can't say that word! You can't swim that way!
That bubble was VIOLENT! This current's NOT SAFE!
You're swimming too fast! You're swimming too slow!
Oh great, now THIS fish just ruined the flow!'

The fish were confused. 'What did we do?'
Woke Fish just screamed, 'THAT'S PRIVILEGE FOR YOU!
You need to be better! You need to reflect!
Now say you're a bad fish and show some respect!'

Some fish just nodded, they just played along...
They figured it best if they didn't swim wrong.
'Agree with the Woke Fish, don't argue, don't fight...
Just say you're the problem, and you'll be all right!'

And way in the back, where the seaweed grew thick,
One fish just sat there, just clicking and clicked.
Its head was down low, its fins didn't move...
It didn't even notice the rest of the school!

'Hey, Doomscroll Fish! The ocean's a mess!'
But Doomscroll Fish just scrolled and said, 'Yes...
Look at this vid! A fish doing a dance!
Wait—what's this fight? Oh, I don't have a chance...'

'I'm watching a trend! It's got so many views!
Oh shit, I just missed the biggest fish news!
Wait—who's mad at who?! Who's canceled today?!
Ah, fuck it, I'll just check InstaFish anyway.'

'What should I do?!' cried Trend Fish one day,
'I don't have a thought—I just do what they say!
If the Woke Fish is woke, then I must be, too!
If the Black Fish is mad, then I must be blue!'

'I must be on trend, I must follow the lead!
So tell me what's right and tell me what's ME!
Do I swim left?! Do I swim right?!
OH FUCK, WHAT'S TRENDING?! I'LL CHANGE OVERNIGHT!'

One day he was purple, the next he was green,
One day he swam proud, the next he felt mean.
One day he screamed, 'We must protect the sand!
It's being OPPRESSED! IT DESERVES TO STAND!'

'Ban seaweed FOREVER!' he raged for a week…
'Oh wait, seaweed's BACK?! Shit, I'll delete that tweet!
I'm anti-bubbles! They're problematic too!
No wait—bubbles are IN?! THEN I LOVE THEM, WOOHOO!'

Trend Fish just panicked, afraid to be wrong,
So he copied, he followed, and swam right along.
'I don't have a thought! I don't have a clue!
Just TELL me what's right, and I'll do what YOU do!'

Then swooped a shadow, a mouth full of teeth,
A shark who had come from the depths underneath.
'Oh yes!' said the shark, 'This is just what I need!
A sea full of FISH who are angry indeed!'

'Keep up the fighting! Keep up the hate!
The more you divide, the more you'll need ME, mate!
You need a strong leader! You need a great cause!
Now bow to my wisdom... and give me applause!'

Then he pulled out a banner, big, shiny, and bright,
With bold, giant letters in black and in white:
"SHARK LIVES MATTER—WE'RE HUNTED AND FEARED!"
'We sharks are the victims! Our pain is severe!'

'Donate to my movement! Wear one of my tees!
Shout it out loud: "NO JUSTICE, NO SEAS!"
Get the stickers! Get the hats! Get the signs and the books!
And if you don't buy them... well, that's kinda sus.'

'I'll fight for the weak! I'll fight for the small!
But first, you must fight each other—that's all!
Keep up the chaos! Keep taking the bait!
And while you all argue, I'LL BE THE GREAT!'

Then, with a grin, he swam through the schools,
Whispering softly, 'I make all the rules...'

The ocean once open, the ocean once free,
Now had new laws for how fish must be.
'You swim with your color, your label, your type—
If you disagree, then you aren't 'doing it right!"

'Stay in your lane!' cried the fish in their schools,
'Swim with YOUR kind! These are the new rules!'
And fish who once played, fish who had fun,
Now watched their old friends get shamed one by one.

'You're swimming too close! You're swimming too wide!'
'Your bubbles are wrong! You must pick a side!'
'Your fins are offensive! Your tail's kinda rude!'
'Apologize now—or be CANCELED, fool!'

Some fish got nervous. Some fish felt small.
Some fish just shrugged and said, 'Fine, whatever, y'all.'
But deep in their gills, a feeling was there...
Like maybe, just maybe, this shit wasn't so fair...

But THEN, in the schools, a fight had begun...
The Woke Fish had FINALLY turned on its own!
'YOU'RE not woke enough!' one fish yelled with glee,
'You said something WRONG back in Year 43!'

'What? No, I didn't!' cried Woke Fish in fear,
'I've ALWAYS been perfect! I'VE ALWAYS BEEN CLEAR!'
But the fish pulled up records, old bubbles, old chats—
'EXPOSED!' they all shouted. 'You once SWAM WITH WHITES!'

'I—I didn't mean to! It was back in my youth!'
'That doesn't matter! You must face the truth!
You're OUT! You're done! You're CANCELED TODAY!
You tried to lead, but you SWAM THE WRONG WAY!'

And so Woke Fish, once strong, once so bold,
Was now left alone, abandoned, controlled.
'WAIT!' Woke Fish cried. 'THIS ISN'T THE PLAN!'
But the rules had been set... and no one gave a damn.

And all through the madness, as schools tore apart...
As fish screamed and pointed and fought from the heart...
As friendships were broken, as schools split in two...
One fish stayed silent, without any clue.

Floating in an abyss, in a glow soft and blue...
Doomscroll Fish continued to scroll, like dumb fish often do...
'Wow, a shrimp learned to juggle! I gotta retweet!
And holy shit—THIS PUFFER JUST BOUNCED TO A BEAT!'

The fish world was drowning in fighting and fear,
But Doomscroll Fish? He didn't hear.
For he was too lost in his digital feed—
Watching a lobster review different seaweed.

'Damn, this trend is gonna go viral!
Wait—WTF? Why are fish in a spiral?
Oh wow, the ocean's collapsing? No way...
#SendingThoughtsAndBubbles. Hooray.'

Deep in the waters, the shark gave a grin...
'My work here is done, my victory's in!
They fought and they screamed! They pushed and they shoved!
And ALL that it took was a WHISPER of hate!'

'They needed a leader! They needed a guide!
But what they don't know... is they're ALL on my side!
I made all the rules! I made all the fights!
And soon, very soon... I'LL TAKE THE FIRST BITE!'

Then, with a laugh, he circled the schools...
Fat from the chaos... and making new rules...

He held up a scroll, with 'Laws of the Sea'—
'Approved by the Fish!' (But written by me).
The fish leaned in close, their fins held polite,
Not seeing his grin... or his jaw lock tight.

Off in the distance, one fish looked around...
And FINALLY noticed what dark truth he'd found.
The fighting, the rage, the rules and the fear...
Had all been designed to bring SHARKS over here.

'Wait... we're divided, we're weak, we're blind...
And HOLY SHIT—THERE'S A SHARK BEHIND!
We fell for the bait! We let him take hold!
AND NOW WE'RE JUST WAITING... TO GET OUR ASSES SOLD!'

He turned to his friends, but they didn't agree...
'Shhh! Don't say that! That sounds kinda extreme!'
'Besides, we must focus! The real threat's not him!'
'It's the fish over THERE who don't think right within!'

The shark licked his teeth, the schools just kept fighting...
And one fish swam backward... a little too frightened...

And just like that, with a flick of his fin…
The Shark grinned wide and said, 'Let's begin.'
The schools were still bickering, still slinging blame…
So nobody noticed when the first fish got maimed.

One chomp. Two chomps. Then three, then four…
The Shark had his feast while they yelled even more!
'You SWAM in my space!' 'You USED the wrong word!'
'You DIDN'T repost! You're part of the herd!'

They fought and they screamed! They kept up the show!
And nobody noticed their numbers got low.
'We must do better! We must be strong!
Now let's take a vote on what words feel wrong!'

And deep in the blue, with a belly so round...
The Shark simply chuckled and gulped the next down...

The fish stood there frozen, their fins feeling weak...
Too stunned to fight, too frightened to speak.
The Shark stretched and grinned, then gave a small yawn...
'I'd eat a few more... but I think I'll move on.'

'You'll rebuild, you'll regroup, you'll start fresh and new!
You'll rewrite new rules, make a brand new mistake—
You'll dress it in kindness, in progress, in grace...
And when it all breaks... I'll be there to partake.'

They'd argued and posted, they'd virtue-signaled loud—
But none of that mattered now under the shroud.
For truth isn't viral, and peace isn't praised...
And predators thrive when good fish look dazed.

'Oh no! Oh HELP! Oh WHAT HAVE WE DONE?!
Shark, tell us how we can make this undone!'
The Shark simply laughed, his teeth shining bright...
'Oh nothing, my friends. You just lost the fight.'

And far down below, the ocean rolled on...
It cared not for bubbles, it cared not for brawls.
For water is water, it's always the same—
It doesn't pick sides, it doesn't take names.

But fish? Oh, fish—they swim and they fight...
They build up their schools, they always think they are right.
And long after this, when new fish arrive...
Will THEY make it better? Or keep hate alive?

So tell me, dear reader, what WILL you do?
Will you fall for the tricks? Will you swim with your school?
Will you fight with your friends? Will you cancel your peers?
Or will you wake up... and swim on your own without fear?

Now that you've read it, don't just drift past—
Are you thinking for real... or stuck in a cast?
The choice is all yours, as you float in the sea...
Just don't be the fish who gets played—like most tend to be.